Written by Rosie Greening.
Illustrated by Stuart Lynch.

# We are the grOOvicOrns!

**ROSIE GREENING ★ STUART LYNCH**

make
believe
ideas

Everyone **loves** unicorns. They always make a fuss.
But you know who **should** be famous?

but make
amazing
slides!

# Unicorns sign hoofprints,

My Unicorn Scrapbook

To Rabbit, Love Glitter

HAPPY BIRTHDAY

We don't have
magic powers,

but we still make **dreams** come true!

We have **MUlticoloured** tents

All Welcome

The unicorns
**bring**
**sunshine**
everywhere
they go.

The sun is **super boring.**
You know what's better?

# SNOW!

The unicorns are bigheads –
they **SHOW OFF** all day long.

Glow 'n' go
hoof polish

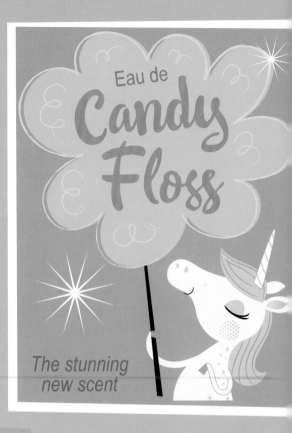

Eau de
Candy
Floss

*The stunning
new scent*

Who would
want to smell
like candy floss?

The snooty
unicorns,
that's who!

They **never** want to play with us, and — HEY!

You've got it wrong.

Mane-gain!

Grow luscious locks in minutes

They're not THAT bad...

It's **hard** to be a
**unicorn** –
we have a **lot** to do.

There's **never**
any time to play.
We wish we were
like **YOU!**

To Do
Make rainbow
*
Grant wish
*
Rainbow school
*
Hoofprint signing
*
Mane maintenance
*
Polish hooves
*
Attend premiere